05/2006

D0093503

DISCARDED

Young Cam Jansen
and the
Spotted Cat Mystery

A Viking Easy-to-Read

BY DAVID A. ADLER

ILLUSTRATED BY SUSANNA NATTI

VIKING

For Netanel, Emunah, Avital, and Techiya
—D.A.

To Ding-guo, Sue-Hwa, Qing, Jeff, and Stephanie
—S.N.

VIKING
Published by Penguin Group
Penguin Young Readers Group, 345 Hudson Street, New York, New York 10014, U.S.A.
Penguin Group (Canada), 90 Eglinton Avenue East, Suite 700, Toronto, Ontario, Canada M4P 2Y3
(a division of Pearson Penguin Canada Inc.)
Penguin Books Ltd, 80 Strand, London WC2R 0RL, England
Penguin Ireland, 25 St Stephen's Green, Dublin 2, Ireland (a division of Penguin Books Ltd)
Penguin Group (Australia), 250 Camberwell Road, Camberwell, Victoria 3124, Australia
(a division of Pearson Australia Group Pty Ltd)
Penguin Books India Pvt Ltd, 11 Community Centre, Panchsheel Park, New Delhi – 110 017, India
Penguin Group (NZ), Cnr Airborne and Rosedale Roads, Albany, Auckland 1310, New Zealand
(a division of Pearson New Zealand Ltd)
Penguin Books (South Africa) (Pty) Ltd, 24 Sturdee Avenue, Rosebank, Johannesburg 2196, South Africa

Penguin Books Ltd, Registered Offices: 80 Strand, London WC2R 0RL, England

First published in 2006 by Viking, a division of Penguin Young Readers Group

1 3 5 7 9 10 8 6 4 2

Text copyright © David A. Adler, 2006
Illustrations copyright © Susanna Natti, 2006
All rights reserved

LIBRARY OF CONGRESS CATALOGING-IN-PUBLICATION DATA
Adler, David A.
Young Cam Jansen and the spotted cat mystery / by David A. Adler ; illustrated by Susanna Natti.
p. cm. — (Young Cam Jansen ; 12)
Summary: When a cat appears in their classroom one rainy day,
Cam and her friend Eric figure out where it came from.
ISBN 0-670-06094-1 (hardcover)
[1. Cats—Fiction. 2. Schools—Fiction. 3. Mystery and detective stories.]
I. Natti, Susanna, ill. II. Title.
PZ7.A2615Yu 2006
[Fic]—dc22
2005034006

Viking® and Easy-to-Read® are registered trademarks of Penguin Group (USA) Inc.

Manufactured in China
Set in Bookman

CONTENTS

1. MEOW! MEOW!

"Please, walk on the mat,"

Mrs. Wayne, the principal's assistant,

called out.

"Wipe your boots."

It was a cold, rainy day.

Cam Jansen and her friend Eric Shelton

walked into school.

They wiped their boots on the mat.

"Aren't you that clicking girl?"

Mrs. Wayne asked.

Cam smiled. "I say 'Click!'

when I want to remember something."

Eric smiled, too.

He told Mrs. Wayne,

"Cam remembers whatever she sees.

It's as if she has a camera in her head

and lots of pictures.

That's why she says, 'Click!'

That's the sound a camera makes."

"Turn around," Mrs. Wayne told Cam.

"Tell me what I'm wearing."

Cam turned. "Click!" she said,

and closed her eyes.

"You're wearing boots."

"Of course I am," Mrs. Wayne said.

"It's cold and raining outside."

"There's an oak leaf

on the toe of your left boot," Cam said.

"The tip of the leaf is torn."

Mrs. Wayne looked at her boot.

"Oh, my! You're right," she said,

and took the leaf off her boot.

Cam's real name is Jennifer,

but when people found out

about her great memory,

they called her "The Camera."

Then "The Camera" became just "Cam."

"You're amazing!" Mrs. Wayne said.

"You really do have a great memory."

Cam opened her eyes.

Then she walked with Eric to class.

Their teacher, Ms. Dee,

was standing in the hall,

right by the door to their classroom.

"Good morning," Ms. Dee said. "You're early."

"My mom didn't want us

to wait in the rain for the bus," Cam said.

"She drove us here."

"Please," Ms. Dee said,

"take off your raincoats and boots.

Get ready for class."

Cam and Eric walked into the room.

They were the first children in class.

The room was neat.

The floor was clean.

They took off their coats.

Cam helped Eric take his boots off.

Eric helped Cam take her boots off.

They went to the back of the room

and hung their coats on hooks.

"Hey," Eric said. "Look in the corner.

Danny forgot his sweater."

Eric went to pick it up

and something moved.

"Meow! Meow!"

A white cat

with a large black spot on its tail

ran from the corner

and hid beneath Ms. Dee's desk.

2. THE CAT'S NAME IS *SPOTTY*

"Good morning," Beth said

as she walked into the classroom.

Jane, Tim, and Danny walked in, too.

"I love the rain," Danny said.

He spun around.

Water sprayed off his raincoat.

"Hey!" Beth shouted.

"You got me wet!"

"Water is good for you," Danny said.

"It makes plants grow."

"Well, I'm not a plant!"

More children walked into the room.

Danny dropped his books on the floor.

His homework papers fell out.

He shook his boots.

Water splashed off them

and hit the cat. *"Meow!"*

The cat ran from Ms. Dee's desk.

It ran across Danny's books and papers.

It ran back to the coat corner

and into Danny's sweater.

"Whose cat is that?" Danny asked.

"We found it here this morning," Cam said.

"Look," Danny called to Ms. Dee.

"Cam brought a cat to school."

Ms. Dee walked into the room.

"There it is," Danny said, and pointed.

"Oh, how sweet," Ms. Dee said.

She held out her arms.

"Come here," she said softly.

The cat looked at Ms. Dee.

"Come here," Ms. Dee said again.

The cat ran into her arms.

Ms. Dee petted the cat.

Then she told Cam,

"You can't keep a cat in school.

You'll have to call your mother

to come and take it home."

"But it's not my cat," Cam said.

Danny laughed.

He pointed at Cam and sang,

"Cam Jansen has a little cat.

Its fleece is white as snow.

It followed Cam to school one day.

Ms. Dee said it must go."

"That's not funny," Cam said. "It's not my cat."

"We found it in the coat corner," Eric said,

"in Danny's sweater."

"Well, it's not my cat," Danny said.

"I don't have any pets."

"Then whose cat is it?" Ms. Dee asked.

No one answered.

"The cat has a collar," Beth said.

Ms. Dee held the cat up.

A small brass tag hung from its collar.

Ms. Dee looked at it and said,

"The cat's name is *Spotty*."

3. SOMETHING STRANGE

"I'll make 'Lost Cat' signs," Danny said.

"We can put them on trees."

Beth said, "First we should give Spotty

something to eat and drink."

"I have a can of tuna for lunch,"

Ms. Dee said.

"I'll share it with Spotty."

Ms. Dee put Spotty on the floor by her desk.

She opened her lunch bag

and took out a small can of tuna fish.

Ms. Dee put a sheet of paper on the floor.

She opened the can.

Then she spilled some tuna fish

onto the paper.

"It's for you," Ms. Dee told Spotty.

Spotty purred.

But Spotty didn't eat the fish.

"I have some water," Eric said.

"And I have a bowl," Ms. Dee added.

Eric took a small bottle of water

from his lunch bag.

Ms. Dee took a bowl from her closet.

She set it beside the tuna fish.

Eric poured some water into the bowl.

Beth stood beside the fish and water.

"Here, Spotty," Beth said.

"You must be hungry."

Spotty didn't run to the food and water.

It ran into Beth's arms.

Cam looked at Spotty.

Then she looked at Danny's papers.

Cam closed her eyes and said, "Click!"

"Go on," Beth told Spotty.

"Eat some fish. Drink some water."

But Spotty just looked up at Beth and purred.

"I'm done," Danny said.

He held up a sheet of paper.

Are you looking for me?

was on the top of the paper.

Beneath that was a picture.

"That's not a picture of Spotty," Beth said.

"It looks like a shoe with feet.

Now who would be looking

for a shoe with feet?"

Cam opened her eyes.

"Look at my sign," Danny said.

"Yes," Beth said. "Look at it.

Does that look like Spotty?"

Cam looked at the sign.

"It's very nice," Cam said,

"but I don't think we need that sign.

Look at Danny's other papers—

the ones on the floor."

"Hey," Danny said. "That's my homework."

"There's something strange

about those papers," Cam said.

"Something is missing from them."

4. CAM JANSEN CLICKED!

Danny looked at his homework papers.

"There's nothing missing," he said.

"I answered every question."

Eric looked at Danny's homework.

"Name the world's five oceans," Eric read.

Then he read Danny's answer.

"George, Fred, Nancy, Jacob, and Beth."

"Hey," Beth said. "I'm not an ocean.

George, Fred, Nancy, and Jacob

are also *not* names of oceans.

Those are names of people."

21

"The world's five oceans," Eric said,

"are Atlantic, Pacific, Indian, Arctic,

and Antarctic."

Ms. Dee looked at Danny's homework.

"All your math answers are wrong, too,"

Ms. Dee said.

Cam said, "The right answers are not

all that's missing from Danny's homework.

Spotty walked across those papers twice.

What's missing are Spotty's wet paw prints."

"Yes," Ms. Dee said.

"There are no paw prints."

"I clicked," Cam said, "and looked at

the picture I have in my head of the floor when we came into the room.

The floor was clean. If Spotty came here from outside the school," Cam said, "there would have been lots of wet paw prints on the floor."

"Maybe he came in yesterday," Beth said.

Cam shook her head again.

"If Spotty came here last night before the rain, then he would have been hungry."

Ms. Dee asked Cam, "When do you think Spotty came to school?"

Cam smiled. "I think Spotty lives here. Spotty lives in the school."

5. THE REWARD I WANT

"Let's ask Mrs. Wayne," Eric said.

"She would know if a class has a pet cat."

"Eric, that's a good idea," Ms. Dee said.

"You and Cam should go, and, of course, Beth.

Spotty seems to like her."

Beth was still holding Spotty.

"What about me?" Danny asked.

Ms. Dee told Danny, "You need to stay here.

You think there's an ocean named George."

Ms. Dee read from his math paper.

"I asked, 'How much are four apples

plus three apples plus two apples?'"

"Nine!" Eric said.

"Danny wrote, 'That's a lot of fruit.'"

Danny laughed.

Ms. Dee didn't.

She said, "You'll stay here

and do your homework again."

Cam, Eric, and Beth left the room.

They walked toward the front hall.

Eric said, "The kindergarten classes have pets.

They have fish and hamsters."

"But they don't have a cat," Cam said.

"They wouldn't. Cats eat fish and hamsters."

Cam stopped.

"Oh, my," she said. "That's it."

Cam started to walk the other way.

"Follow me," she said.

They walked to the back hall.

"Cats don't only eat fish and hamsters.

They eat mice.

Lots of stores have cats

to keep mice away."

Cam stopped at the custodian's door.

She knocked on it.

"Who is it?" Mrs. Adams asked.

"It's me," Cam said, "Cam Jansen."

"Come in," Mrs. Adams said.

Cam opened the door.

"Spotty!" Mrs. Adams said.

"Where were you?"

Spotty jumped from Beth

and into Mrs. Adams's arms.

Mrs. Adams told Cam, Eric, and Beth,

"A few years ago, the gym teacher

came in here all upset.

He saw mice in the gym.

That's when I got Spotty.

She chased the mice out.

Now I just love her.

But I'm careful.

Some children are allergic to cats.

Spotty might scare some of the pets

in the kindergarten classes.

I was so busy all morning mopping up puddles.

I must have left my door open

and Spotty got out."

Beth said, "We found Spotty in our classroom.

We didn't know how she got there."

"Cam solved the mystery," Eric said.

"Please," Mrs. Adams said,

"take pretzels and juice as a reward."

Cam and Eric each took a pretzel

from the bowl on Mrs. Adams's desk.

"I would like to come here

and visit Spotty," Beth said.

"That's the reward I want."

Spotty purred.

"Eric and I would like to visit, too," Cam said.

"Spotty and I would like that," Mrs. Adams said.

"Visit us after lunch."

There was a knock on the door.

Mrs. Wayne came into the office.

"Some children didn't wipe their feet

on the mat," Mrs. Wayne said.

"There's a puddle in the front hall."

Mrs. Adams told Cam, Eric, and Beth,

"I need to go to work."

"We need to go to class," Eric said.

"I'll walk with you,"

Mrs. Wayne told the children.

When they were in the hall,

Mrs. Wayne told Cam,

"Now, close your eyes and click!"

Cam closed her eyes and clicked!

"Now," Mrs. Wayne said,

"tell me what Mrs. Adams was wearing.

Tell me about the signs on her office walls.

Tell me everything that was on her desk."

Eric and Beth held Cam's hands

as she walked with her eyes closed.

And as she walked,

Cam answered every one

of Mrs. Wayne's questions.

A Cam Jansen
Memory Game

Take another look at the picture on page 4.

Study it.

Blink your eyes and say, "Click!"

Then turn back to this page

and answer these questions:

1. What color is Cam's raincoat? What color is Eric's?
2. Is Cam carrying an umbrella?
3. Who came into school first, Cam or Eric?
4. Is Cam smiling? Is Eric smiling?
5. What color is the floor mat?